This book belongs to:

_____

_____

_____

First published 2001 by Walker Books Ltd
87 Vauxhall Walk, London SE11 5HJ

This edition published 2011

2 4 6 8 10 9 7 5 3 1

© 2001 Lucy Cousins
Lucy Cousins font © 2001 Lucy Cousins

"Maisy" Audio Visual Series produced by King Rollo Films for
Universal Pictures International Visual Programming

Maisy™. Maisy is a registered trademark of Walker Books Ltd, London.

The moral right of the author/illustrator has been asserted

Printed in China

British Library Cataloguing in Publication Data:
a catalogue record for this book is available from the British Library

ISBN 978-1-4063-3480-7

www.walker.co.uk
www.maisyfun.co.uk

Doctor Maisy

Lucy Cousins

WALKER BOOKS
AND SUBSIDIARIES
LONDON • BOSTON • SYDNEY • AUCKLAND

Maisy and Tallulah
are dressing up.
Hello, Doctor Maisy!
Hello, Nurse Tallulah!

Tallulah listens to Maisy's heartbeat.

Baboom, baboom!

Ha-ha, that tickles!

Panda feels ill.
Maisy listens to
his heartbeat.

Baboom, baboom!

Maisy checks
Panda's temperature.
Poor Panda –
he's very hot.

Maisy takes Panda upstairs and puts him to bed.

There, there, Panda. Get well soon.

Oh, Maisy, is that Tallulah calling?

Don't run on
the stairs, Maisy.

Watch out,
Tallulah...

Oops!

Tallulah is all right, but Maisy has hurt her nose.

Nurse Tallulah
wraps Maisy's nose
in a bandage.

There, that's better!
Bye-bye, Nurse Tallulah.
Bye-bye, Doctor Maisy.

Read and enjoy the Maisy story books

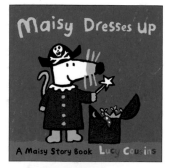
Maisy Dresses up
A Maisy Story Book Lucy Cousins

Maisy's Bedtime
A Maisy Story Book Lucy Cousins

Maisy's Pool
A Maisy Story Book Lucy Cousins

Maisy Makes Lemonade
A Maisy Story Book Lucy Cousins

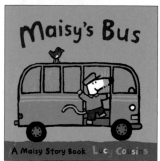
Maisy's Bus
A Maisy Story Book Lucy Cousins

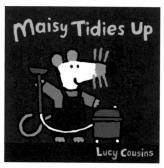
Maisy Tidies Up
Lucy Cousins

Maisy Makes Gingerbread
A Maisy Story Book Lucy Cousins

Maisy's Bathtime
A Maisy Story Book Lucy Cousins

My friend Maisy

Doctor Maisy
A Maisy Story Book Lucy Cousins

Maisy Goes Shopping
A Maisy Story Book Lucy Cousins

Available from all good booksellers

It's more fun with Maisy!